The Rocking Chair

Contents

1

The Junk Shop

Ray loved junk shops.
So did his girlfriend Jackie.
They loved nosing about in them,
looking for bargains.
They were junk shop junkies.

On Sundays, they used to drive out
into the country,
to small villages and market towns,
looking for junk shops.

Sometimes they picked up bargains.
Sometimes they found nothing,
but they didn't really mind.
It was fun just looking.

Ray used to say that one day
they would find something really special.
Something out of the ordinary.
But they never had.

Until the day they found the rocking chair.
That was out of the ordinary all right.

It was a Sunday and they had driven out
to a small market town.
They couldn't find any junk shops at first.
Then, at last, they spotted one
in a quiet little street.

It was a dark, dirty, dusty little shop.
The things in the window
didn't look very special.
There was an old clock with no hands.
An old violin with no strings.
And an old china doll with no hair.

Jackie shivered.
'I don't like this place,' she said. 'Let's go.'
'Don't be silly!' said Ray.
'You never know what's inside.
This could be the place
where we find something really special.'

He pushed open the door.
A bell rang.
Ray disappeared into the dark little shop.
Jackie shivered again.
Then she followed him in.

2

The Rocking Chair

Inside, it was dark and quiet.
'There's no one here,' whispered Jackie.
'Yes there is,' said a voice.

The owner came out from the back of the shop.
'Can I help you?' he asked
'Just looking, thanks,' said Ray.

There were dusty old books.
Gloomy pictures of landscapes.
Ugly old furniture and a statue of a nun.

Ray touched a tall, carved chair of dark wood.
It moved under his hand.
'It's a rocking chair!' he said.
'Yes, sir,' said the owner. 'A very fine piece.'

Ray looked more closely at the chair.
The carvings were of skulls.
Demons' heads with horns.
The faces of witches and goblins.
'Hey, this is fantastic!
What do you think, Jackie?'
Jackie didn't answer.

'How old is it?' Ray asked the owner.

'Very old,' he said.

'It has rather an interesting history.

The last owner went mad.

Now he sits in a chair and laughs all day,

rocking backwards and forwards.'

'He's gone off his rocker, you mean!' said Ray.

He laughed.

'Yes, sir. One could put it like that.'

'How much is it?'

'A hundred pounds, sir.'

'I'll give you fifty.'

'Seventy-five is my last word, sir.'

'Done!'

'Oh, Ray!' said Jackie.

'Don't buy it! It's horrible!'

'No it isn't,' said Ray. 'It's a very fine piece.

Come on, help me to carry it back to the car.'

The owner stood in the doorway,

watching them go.

3

Is Ray All Right?

The rocking chair was too big to go in the car.
They had to strap it to the roof.

On the way home,
Ray couldn't stop talking about the chair.
'It's a real find,' he said.
'It's something special.
I've never seen one like that before.'

Jackie said nothing.

'Give us a hand to carry it up the stairs,'
said Ray when they got back to his flat.
They put it down in the living-room.
It rocked gently backwards and forwards.

'A lovely piece of work,' said Ray.
'Best seventy-five pounds I've ever spent.'

'I hate it,' said Jackie.
'I feel as if all those faces are looking at me.'
'Don't be silly,' said Ray.
'They're made of wood.
How could they look at you?'

He sat in the chair
and rocked backwards and forwards.
'Fancy you thinking
the faces were looking at you!
Ha ha ha! That's funny, that is!
That's very funny!'
He laughed and laughed and laughed.
His laugh got louder and louder and louder.

'Ray!'
Jackie took him by the arm
and pulled him out of the chair.
'Why are you laughing?'

Ray stopped. 'Was I laughing?'
He looked puzzled. 'I don't know why.
Something just came over me.'

'I've got to go now,' said Jackie.
'Will you be all right?'
'Of course I'll be all right.'
He gave her a kiss. 'See you later.'

After she had gone, Ray sat in the chair again.
Funny, really,
laughing like that over nothing.
Very funny.
Yes, it was very funny indeed . . .

He began to laugh again.

4

The Argument

The next morning, Ray woke up feeling happy.
He went to look at his chair again.

It certainly was a fine piece of work.
He thought about the last owner
and how awful it must be to go mad.

Ray would have liked to sit down in the chair,
but he didn't want to be late for work.

All day at work, he thought about his chair.
He had a chair in the office, of course
but it was made of grey plastic.
It didn't have any faces carved on it.
And it didn't rock.

When he finished work, he rushed home.
He sat in the rocking chair
and rocked backwards and forwards.

This is a real chair, thought Ray, a proper chair.
He had to laugh when he thought of
his grey plastic chair in the office.
Calls itself a chair . . .
Ha ha ha!

There was a knock at the door.
Ray stopped laughing.
How annoying, he thought.
Just when I was enjoying myself!

The knock came again.
He got up and went to the door.

Jackie was standing there.
'Hello,' she said. 'I came to see
if you want to go out for a pizza.'

'A pizza? I don't know.
I was thinking of having a quiet night in.'

'Not so quiet,' said Jackie.
'I heard you laughing just now.'
'So what?' said Ray.
'Can't a man laugh in his own home?'

'OK,' said Jackie. 'I don't want a row.
Let's just go out.'

'Oh, all right,' said Ray.
He didn't really want to go.
But he couldn't think of an excuse.

They went to the local pizza restaurant.
While they were waiting
for the pizzas to arrive,
Ray talked about his chair.

'It's got sixty-six faces on it.
I counted them.'
'Look, Ray,' said Jackie.
'Just shut up about that chair.
It's boring.'
'It's not boring!' said Ray angrily.
'Your trouble is, you're jealous!'
'What? Jealous of a chair?'
'Yes! You're jealous
of my rocking chair!' shouted Ray.

He got up from the table
and walked out of the restaurant.

He went straight home
and sat in his rocking chair.
As he rocked, his bad mood melted away.

He loved his chair.
It never had rows with him.
Never told him off.
Never answered back.
It was a true friend.

5

Jackie Gets Worried

The next day, Ray decided not to go to work.
He wanted to stay at home in his rocking chair.

He phoned up his boss
and said he couldn't come in.
He said he had a bad back.

'All right,' said his boss.
'You get plenty of rest.'

'I will,' said Ray.

All day,
he rocked backwards and forwards in his chair.
He didn't even get out of it for lunch.
He just wanted to rock in his chair.
It was so calming . . . so soothing . . .

Towards the evening, the telephone rang.
Ray didn't move from his chair.
It was probably Jackie.
He just let the phone ring and ring.
It rang for five minutes, then stopped.
Ray smiled.

An hour later, there was a knock at the door
Ray still didn't move from his chair.
He knew it was Jackie.
Why couldn't she leave him alone?

The knocking went on and on.
Then Ray heard Jackie's voice,
shouting through the letter-box.

'Ray? Are you there?'

Ray didn't answer.
He could just imagine how silly she looked,
bending down to shout through the letter-box.
He laughed.

'Ray! I can hear you laughing!
Answer the door – I'm worried about you!'

But Ray didn't answer the door.
He just carried on rocking and laughing.

And in the end, Jackie went away.

6

Sacked!

After that, Ray stopped going to work.
He spent all day rocking in his chair.
Sometimes the telephone rang,
but he never answered it.

One day a letter came from his boss.
It told him he'd got the sack.
Ray didn't care.
He screwed the letter up and threw it away.
Then he went back to his chair.

He hardly ever went out.
Sometimes he went out to the shops
to get some food, but not very often.
As time went by, he did it less and less.
He didn't feel much like eating these days.
Which was just as well –
now that he'd lost his job
he had no money for food.
It was quite neat, really.
He'd lost his job and his appetite
at the same time.

There was something quite funny about that.
Thinking about it,
as he rocked away in his chair,
Ray began to laugh.

Days went by like this.
Ray stayed at home,
rocking in his chair
and laughing to himself,
not answering the phone or the door,
even when Jackie called.

He stopped washing and shaving.
A thick beard covered his face.

He hardly ate anything.
He got so thin, he looked like a skeleton.
A skeleton with a beard.

Then one day he heard banging at the door.
He didn't answer.
He just carried on rocking.

Then he heard Jackie's voice.
'If you don't open the door, Ray,
I'm going to smash it down.'

'Go away!' called Ray.
He was surprised at the sound of his voice –
it sounded weak and thin,
not like his own voice at all.
He didn't know if she could even hear him.

But he could hear her all right.
The next minute,
there was a smashing, splintering sound.
Then the sound of the front door swinging open.
Then Jackie's footsteps in the hall.

She came into the room.
She was holding an axe.

7

The Axe

'Oh no, Ray!' said Jackie.

'What's happened to you?'

'Nothing,' said Ray. 'I'm all right.'

'But you're so thin! And it stinks in here –
when did you last have a bath?'

'None of your business.
Just go away. Leave us alone.'

'What do you mean, *us*?' asked Jackie.

'Me and my chair, of course,' answered Ray.

'Right, that's it,' said Jackie.

'Get out of that chair.

I'm going to smash it.'

'No, you're not,' said Ray.

He closed his eyes.

'When I open my eyes, you'll be gone.'

'Ray – you're off your rocker!'

'No, I'm not,' said Ray, opening his eyes.

'I'm on my rocker – and I'm not getting off!'

That was a good joke, thought Ray.

On my rocker.

He started to laugh.

Jackie swung the axe.

It bit deep into the leg of the chair.

Ray screamed

as if the axe had bitten into his own leg.

He jumped out of the chair.

Jackie raised the axe high.

'Goodbye, rocking chair,' she said.

8

The Accident

'No!' shouted Ray.
He had to save his rocking chair.
He made a grab for the axe.
He was weak from lack of food,
but anger made him strong.

He twisted the axe out of Jackie's hands
and hit her with it.
Not with the sharp blade.
Just with the back of the handle.

He didn't want to hurt her
just get rid of her.
But he must have hit harder
than he had meant to.
Jackie went down and didn't get up.

Ray stared at her.
She didn't move.
What had he done?
He had killed someone.
He was . . . a murderer.

A horrible cold feeling ran through him.
He had come back to his senses.
'I didn't mean to,' he said aloud.
'It was an accident, Jackie.'
He began to cry.

He sank back into the chair.
He rocked backwards and forwards,
still crying.

27

After a while, he stopped crying.

As he rocked, he began to see the funny side.

Jackie had come round with an axe

to smash up his chair.

Well, it wasn't the chair that got smashed up,

was it?

It was Jackie –

the person who'd brought the axe along

in the first place!

That was quite funny, really.

He began to laugh.

And that was how the police found them

when they came into the flat two days later.

Jackie lay dead on the floor.

Nearby, Ray rocked backwards and forwards

in his chair,

laughing his head off.